POP!
and
Mum Has a Ban

Written by
William Anthony

Illustrated by
Brandon Mattless

Can you say this sound and draw it with your finger?

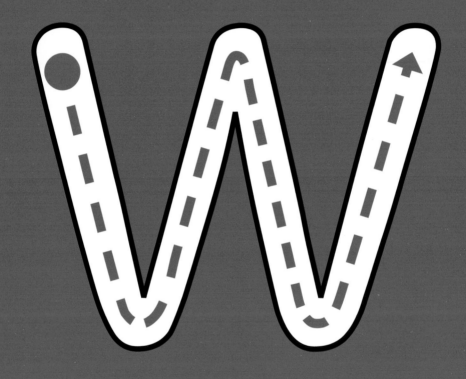

POP!

Written by
William Anthony

Illustrated by
Brandon Mattless

Mum has the jug.

Puff! The jug is on Nan.

Mum has the wig.

Puff! The wig is on Nan.

Mum has the van.

Puff! The van is on Nan.

Mum has the jet.

Puff! The jet is on Nan.

Mum has the...

"No, Mum! It will go—"

POP!

Can you say this sound and draw it with your finger?

Mum Has a Ban

Written by
William Anthony

Illustrated by
Brandon Mattless

Nan is mad. Mum is bad.

Mum has a ban.

"Can we go and jog, Nan?"

Kim and Meg can.
Mum can not.

"Can we go and jam, Nan?"

Kim and Meg can.
Mum can not.

"Can we get wet, Nan?"

Kim and Meg can.
Mum can not.

"Can we fill the jug, Nan?"

Kim and Meg can.
Mum can not.

"Kim, no! The jug!"
"We can mop up, Nan."

"No, Mum can!"

©2021 **BookLife Publishing Ltd.**
King's Lynn, Norfolk PE30 4LS

ISBN 978-1-83927-428-2

POP! & Mum Has a Ban
Written by William Anthony
Illustrated by Brandon Mattless

An Introduction to BookLife Readers...

Our Readers have been specifically created in line with the London Institute of Education's approach to book banding and are phonetically decodable and ordered to support each phase of Letters and Sounds.

Each book has been created to provide the best possible reading and learning experience. Our aim is to share our love of books with children, providing both emerging readers and prolific page-turners with beautiful books that are guaranteed to provoke interest and learning, regardless of ability.

BOOK BAND GRADED using the Institute of Education's approach to levelling.

PHONETICALLY DECODABLE supporting each phase of Letters and Sounds.

EXERCISES AND QUESTIONS to offer reinforcement and to ascertain comprehension.

BEAUTIFULLY ILLUSTRATED to inspire and provoke engagement, providing a variety of styles for the reader to enjoy whilst reading through the series.

AUTHOR INSIGHT:
WILLIAM ANTHONY

Despite his young age, William Anthony's involvement with children's education is quite extensive. He has written over 60 titles with BookLife Publishing so far, across a wide range of subjects. William graduated from Cardiff University with a 1st Class BA (Hons) in Journalism, Media and Culture, creating an app and a TV series, among other things, during his time there.

William Anthony has also produced work for the Prince's Trust, a charity created by HRH The Prince of Wales, that helps young people with their professional future. He has created animated videos for a children's education company that works closely with the charity.

PHASE 2 AND 3
/j/v/w/

This book focuses on the phonemes /j/, /v/ and /w/ and is a red level 2 book band.

Helpful Hints for Reading at Home

The graphemes (written letters) and phonemes (units of sound) used throughout this series are aligned with Letters and Sounds. This offers a consistent approach to learning whether reading at home or in the classroom.

HERE IS A LIST OF PHONEMES FOR THIS PHASE OF LEARNING. AN EXAMPLE OF THE PRONUNCIATION CAN BE FOUND IN BRACKETS.

Phase 2			
s (sat)	a (cat)	t (tap)	p (tap)
i (pin)	n (net)	m (man)	d (dog)
g (go)	o (sock)	c (cat)	k (kin)
ck (sack)	e (elf)	u (up)	r (rabbit)
h (hut)	b (ball)	f (fish)	ff (off)
l (lip)	ll (ball)	ss (hiss)	

Phase 3 Set 6			
j (jam)	v (van)	w (win)	x (mix)

Phase 3 Set 7			
y (yellow)	z (zoo)	zz (buzz)	qu (quick)

HERE ARE SOME WORDS WHICH YOUR CHILD MAY FIND TRICKY.

Phase 2 Tricky Words			
the	to	I	no
go	into		

Phase 3 Tricky Words			
he	you	she	they
we	all	me	are
be	my	was	her

GPC focus: /j/v/w/

TOP TIPS FOR HELPING YOUR CHILD TO READ:

- Allow children time to break down unfamiliar words into units of sound and then encourage children to string these sounds together to create the word.

- Encourage your child to point out any focus phonics when they are used.

- Read through the book more than once to grow confidence.

- Ask simple questions about the text to assess understanding.

- Encourage children to use illustrations as prompts.

PHASE 2 AND 3

/j/v/w/

This book focuses on the phonemes /j/, /v/ and /w/ and is a red level 2 book band.

9018237302

POP!
and
Mum Has a Ban

PHASE 2 AND 3

/j/v/w/

Level 2 – Red

BookLife
Readers